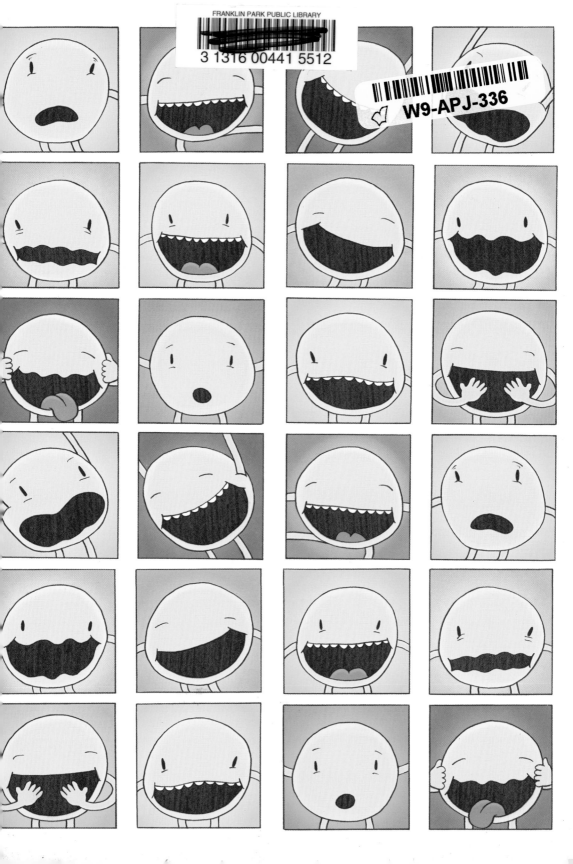

A JUMP•INTO•CHAPTERS Book™

Copyright © 2014 Michael Townsend
All rights reserved/CIP data is available. Published in the United States 2014 by
Blue Apple Books, 515 Valley Street, Maplewood, NJ 07040
www.blueapplebooks.com
First Edition 09/14
Printed in China
ISBN: 978-1-60905-458-8 (hardcover edition)
ISBN: 978-1-60905-554-7 (paperback edition)

2 4 6 8 10 9 7 5 3 1

J-GN
MR. BALL
441-5512

MR. BALL

an EGG-cellent Adventure

Michael Townsend

Part 1.
STARTS
HERE

Mr. Ball has a Wild and Scary Idea

Mr. Ball is going to the circus.

He is excited to see the big, wild, scary animals.

Even the high-flyers
did not thrill
Mr. Ball.

Suddenly...

Mr. Ball roared with joy
for the rest of the show.

PART 2.

Mr. Ball is Warned

A Big, Scary, Wild Plan

Step 1: Find a beast.

Step 2: Catch it.

Step 3: Tame it.

Sadly, he was not a bird, but did the Mama-Blob know this?

Mr. Ball quickly got back
in the nest.

He then did his best to
blend in with the mini-blobs

Things got worse for Mr. Ball when dinner arrived.

He was pretty sure he would not like having chewed up worms fed to him.

He was right!

Mr. Ball was trapped, scared, and **SOOO** not hungry.

PART 4.

Mr. Ball Needs Help!!!

They raced through the woods. But would they be too late?

When they arrived...

The Mama bird is teaching her babies to fly!

A short time later, Mr. Ball was cooking up some hot dog

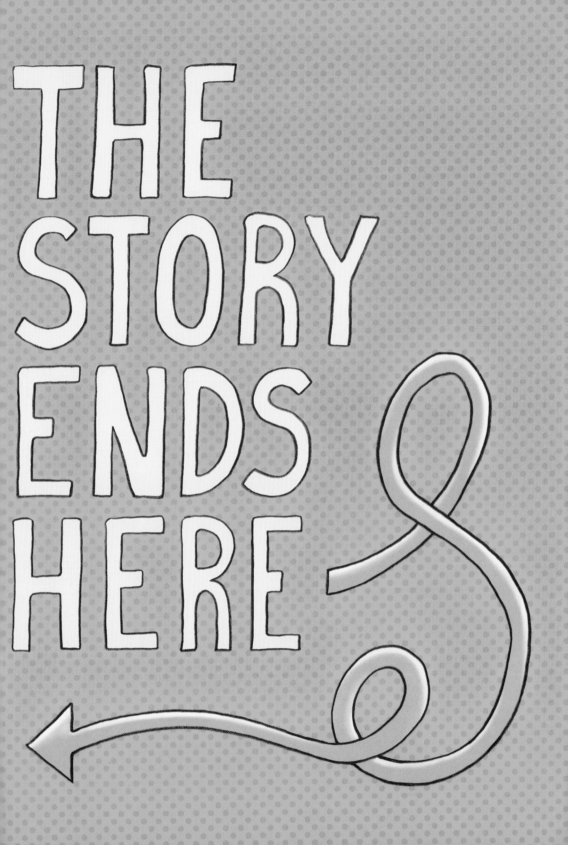

Join us next time when we find out if Tweety Blobs like pie...

Just kidding, the next book will be about Mr. Ball.

But in case you are wondering, Tweety Blobs **do** like pie!

A few seconds later...